THOMAS BAAS

THE FLIGHT
of
MR FINCH

To Nicolas, Osvaldo and Tsentsak.
Thanks to Nora.

T. B.

English edition first published 2018 by order of the Tate Trustees
by Tate Publishing, a division of Tate Enterprises Ltd.,
Millbank, London SW1P 4RG
www.tate.org.uk/publishing
First published in French as *L'envol d'Osvaldo* © Flammarion 2017
This English edition © Tate 2018

A catalogue record for this book is available from the British Library
ISBN 978-1-84976-590-9
Distributed in the United States and Canada by Abrams, New York
Library of Congress Control Number applied for.

Mr Finch

was an ordinary man. Nothing extraordinary ever happened to him. He didn't go on incredible adventures or brave expeditions, and he'd never had a great love story.

To tell you the truth, Mr Finch had never left his neighbourhood. He lived in a small room in the attic of a tall building with his one and only friend, a small bird called Pip.

Each morning, Mr Finch would wake to
the sound of Pip whistling merrily.

With a light heart, Mr Finch would set off
for work. And, when he returned home in
the evening, Pip would greet him eagerly
with a chirp.

They lived very happily like this.

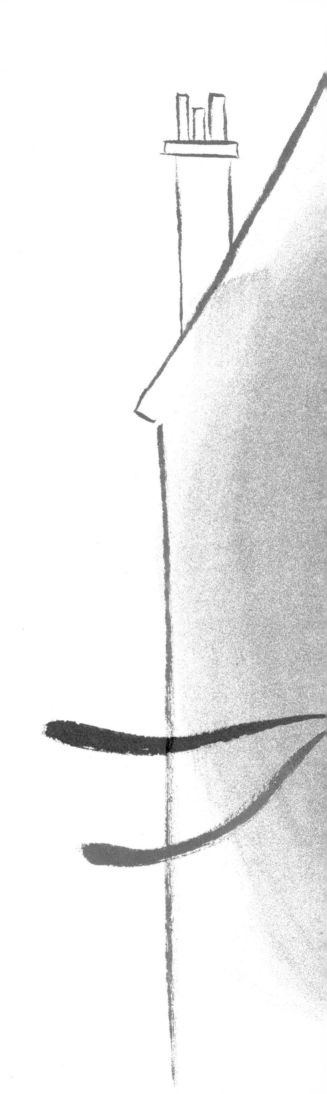

But one morning Pip did not whistle.
And he did not greet Mr Finch with a chirp in the evening.
And there was not a single chirp from him the next day, either.

Pip didn't make any sound at all.

"He must miss the sky,"
thought Mr Finch. So he
put Pip's small cage near
the window, but still his
friend didn't make a sound.

"He must feel cramped,"
said Mr Finch sadly. So he
bought a bigger cage,
but still Pip stayed quiet.

Pip looked unhappy. Mr Finch didn't know what to do.

On his way home the next evening, Mr Finch passed a shop he had never noticed before. It was full of unusual things from strange and exotic lands that he never even knew existed. In the middle of all the jumble, a tiny plant caught his eye.

"That's a very special plant," said the shopkeeper. "It comes from the deepest part of the jungle. It will bring happiness to whomever you give it to."

Delighted by this news, Mr Finch rushed home.
Soon Pip would be whistling again! He placed
the plant next to the cage and waited to see his
friend's reaction.

But there was nothing.
Not one single chirp.
Not even a cheep.
Nothing at all.

The shopkeeper had lied to him. It wasn't a
special plant after all. It was about as magical
as an old green bean.

Just as he did every evening, Mr Finch said
goodnight to his little friend, but Pip didn't
answer. Would he ever chirp again?

The next day, Mr Finch awoke and let out a cry. The small plant had grown so much overnight that his room had been invaded by a jungle!

The cage was lying on the floor with the door flung open.

Pip was gone!

Mr Finch rushed out of the house and down the
stairs, clambering over the plants and vines.

"Pip! Pip! Where are you?" he cried.

Mr Finch

had never been
so far from home.
The plants were dense,
and the noises of the forest were scary.
Everything seemed strange,
from the chatter of unfamiliar birds
to the roars of
wild animals,
which echoed all around him.

"Pip! Piiiiiiiiiip!"

Mr Finch kept calling Pip's name.
He was worried about his friend in this peculiar place.

In the street, it was mayhem. The jungle had taken over the city. People were shouting and running in all directions.

Mr Finch searched desperately for his friend, looking round every corner and peering under every leaf.

He searched and searched, wandering further from home and deeper into the jungle.

As he struggled through the jungle, Mr Finch came face-to-face with a big cat. In truth, it was a jaguar, but Mr Finch didn't know that. He asked timidly, "Have . . . have you seen my small bird go by?"

The impressive beast answered, "If I had seen it, I would have eaten it. There are thousands of birds here. Open your eyes, dear sir!"

Mr Finch continued on his way, troubled by the unhappy thought that his friend could have ended up as the big cat's dinner.

A little further on, Mr Finch met a man at the foot of a gigantic tree.
Mr Finch asked politely, "Excuse me, but have you heard the sound of my
little bird chirping, by any chance?"

The man replied in a wise voice, "If I had heard it, I wouldn't know it was
your bird. There are thousands of birds here. Open your ears, dear sir!"

Mr Finch thanked him and went on his way, straining his ears for
the sound of Pip.

As more time passed, the less progress Mr Finch made. The jungle became denser and closed in around him.

He opened his eyes wide and listened hard, but Pip was nowhere to be found. "He must feel so lonely," thought Mr Finch.

Night was falling, and Mr Finch decided to stop. To his great surprise, he managed to start a fire by rubbing two pieces of wood together. As he warmed himself, he thought about Pip.

Where could he possibly be?
Perched in a snake-infested tree?
In the tummy of a huge beast?

Exhausted by his long journey, Mr Finch fell asleep, soothed by the countless sounds of the jungle.

The next day while washing himself in a river, Mr Finch heard a tiny little chirp. The joyful melody came from the canopy high above.

Mr Finch listened carefully. All of the other noises seemed to disappear.

He recognised Pip's chirping and caught a glimpse of something red at the top of the highest tree.

Mr Finch climbed the tree's enormous trunk. At the top, where the tree touched the sky, he discovered Pip perched on the highest branch.

"Finally, I've found you! I was so worried about you, all alone in this jungle. Let's go back home, my friend!"

The bird thought for a moment, then chirped, "My dear Mr Finch, you wanted me to sing again and you have succeeded. The plant you gave me allowed me to be free. You will always be my friend, but I am much happier here. This is my home."

At first, Mr Finch was very upset, but then he understood Pip's wishes.
All he had ever wanted was for his friend to be happy.

Mr Finch and Pip gave each other a hug and promised to visit regularly.
Then, Mr Finch started his journey back home.

As he sailed away, he began to think about how he had never left his
neighbourhood before, but now he had made this exciting voyage.
He had seen and heard more things in two days than in his entire life!

Back in the city, the jungle had disappeared. Mr Finch walked home. When he opened the door, he saw that the magic plant was still there. He started to clean up the vines and leaves that were lying on the ground.

Pip was happy now, but Mr Finch suddenly felt very lonely.

For the first time, his little room seemed too quiet. He missed the sights and sounds of the jungle.

Lost in his thoughts, Mr Finch jumped when he heard a knock at the door. It was the first time anyone had visited him. His neighbour Clara was standing in his doorway. Mr Finch hadn't really noticed her before, and they had never spoken to each other.

"Dear Mr Finch, you are back! I've been so worried about you. First there were all these plants in the building. Then I heard you calling for Pip, and then you disappeared! I thought I would never see you again."

Mr Finch was surprised that anyone had been worried about him. He began to tell Clara all about his incredible adventure.

"And all of that was thanks to this small plant," Mr Finch concluded. "It helped my friend find true happiness. Now let me give it to you."

Clara took the plant in her hands. Mr Finch smiled. He suddenly felt very happy. Perhaps the plant had worked after all.